S0-ARB-480

The Lizard Hunt

Nancy Robison

Illustrated by
Lynn Munsinger

Lothrop, Lee & Shepard Books
A Division of William Morrow & Co., Inc.
New York

 Inquiries should be addressed to Lothrop, Lee & Shepard Company, 105 Madison Ave., New York, N. Y. 10016.
Printed in the United States of America.

First Edition 1 2 3 4 5 6 7 8 9 10

Library of Congress Cataloging in Publication Data

Robison, Nancy.
The lizard hunt.
SUMMARY: Talley leads her brother into a canyon while hunting lizards. When they become lost, Greg leads them to safety.
[1. Lizards—Fiction. 2. Hunting—Fiction]
I. Munsinger, Lynn. II. Title.
PZ7.R5697Li [E] 78-24374
ISBN 0-688-41875-9 ISBN 0-688-51875-3 lib. bdg.

To Rick and Radcliffe, the world's greatest lizard hunters

Contents

1. How to Catch a Lizard

"This is it!" Talley stopped her bike. "We can find lots of juicy lizards in this canyon!"

Greg stopped behind her. "Why do you want lizards?"

"Mr. Rogers at the pet store said he'd buy all the lizards I can catch." Talley walked away.

Greg followed. "What does Mr. Rogers want with lizards?" He jumped over a large rock.

"He sells them for snake food," Talley said.

"Yuk!" Greg said. "Let's go home and play street hockey!"

"You can do that any time. It's not every day you can go lizard hunting with an expert," Talley said.

"But people get lost in this canyon," Greg said. "The Mountain Search and Rescue Team have to find them."

"Don't be silly," Talley said. "I've been here hundreds of times."

The trail followed a dried-up stream. Talley ran ahead.

"Wait!" Greg called. "Don't go far!"

"Scaredy," she said. "We won't get lost!"

Soon tree branches and bushes covered the trail. Water flowed in the stream.

Talley was fast. Greg had to run to keep up with her.

"Lizards sun themselves on rocks," she said. "Watch where you step."

Greg shouted, "There's one!"

The lizard scampered off.
"Don't yell!" Talley frowned. "You'll scare them away."

She led the way deeper into the canyon.

Greg said, "We're going too far!"

"I know where I'm going," Talley said.

"I hope so." Greg was about to step on a rock when he saw it.

A fat brown lizard was sleeping in the sun.

2.
The Lassoo

"Don't put your foot down,"
Talley whispered.
Greg stood on one foot. He
tried to keep his balance.
He reached out to grab the
lizard by the tail.
Talley stopped him.
"No! Not by the tail. It will
come off and the lizard will
get away!"

"Then how do you catch it?" he asked.

"Don't you know anything?" she said. "Give me a thread."

"I don't have a thread."

"Yes, you do. In your sock.

Pull a thread out of your sock and give it to me."

Greg bent over.

"Why do I listen to you?"

He pulled a long thread from the top of his sock.

"Here."

Talley took the thread.
"Watch. First you tie a loop in the end like this."
She made a small noose with the thread.
"Then you slip it carefully over the lizard's head."

The lizard tried to run. It got caught in the noose.

"You lassooed him!" Greg shouted.

"Now you know how to catch a lizard," Talley said. She held it up carefully to admire it.

"Look at him twist," Greg said. "He'll break that thread and get away!"

"Watch." With her finger, Talley gently rubbed the lizard's belly. The lizard stopped twisting.

"You put it to sleep!" Greg said.

"Right," she said. "Here—you hold him."

"Me?" Greg asked.

"He won't bite. He's asleep." Greg took the end of the thread.

"Pretty neat," he said.

"Too bad that wasn't a blue belly," Talley said. "Blue bellies bring more money."

"Why? Do blue bellies taste better?" Greg asked.

"All lizards are not snake food," she said. "Some are used for other things."

Talley reached in her jeans pocket. She pulled out a cloth bag. Big letters were printed on it:

FIRST NATIONAL BANK

"Where did you get that money bag?" Greg asked.

"Mr. Rogers gave it to me. Money bags are good for keeping lizards."

"How come?" Greg said.

"Because they're made of cloth. Air goes through cloth, and the lizards can breathe," Talley said.

Greg shook his head. "Money bags for lizards! Well, here's your first deposit!"

FIRST

3.
What to Do with a Lizard

"Now that we have this nice fat lizard, can we go?" Greg asked.

Talley tied the bag shut.

"With only one lizard? We need more. Lots more!" Talley handed the bag to Greg. He held it away from him.

Talley disappeared in the brush.

"Come on!"

Greg shouted, “I don’t want to get lost!”

Talley didn’t answer.

Greg took a few steps forward. Talley was on the other side of the stream.

Greg hopped across on the rocks.

“Shh,” she whispered. “Give me a thread.”

“Another one?” Greg asked.

“Hurry, before it gets away.”

On a twig sat a lizard. It looked like a twig itself.

Greg put down the money bag. He pulled a long thread from

his sock. "I'm not going to have a sock left, you know?"

Talley took the thread and lassooed the lizard. Then she rubbed its belly and put it to sleep.

"That was quick," Greg said.

"Of course—I'm an expert," Talley said. "Now open the bag."

"Who, me?" Greg gasped. "The other lizard might jump out!"

"Do I have to do everything?" Talley stared at him.

"Okay." Very carefully, Greg untied the money bag. The lizard inside moved. Greg jumped and dropped the bag.

"Don't let it out!" Talley shouted. She grabbed the bag and closed it.

"Hold it!" she said.

4.
In Search of a Blue Belly

"Two nice fat lizards," Greg said. "Now can we go home?"

"We need more," Talley said.

Greg looked behind him. The trail had disappeared. "I don't like the looks of this," he said. "We're going to get lost."

Talley stooped over.

"Come here," she whispered. "I think I've found a blue belly!"

"How do you know?" Greg whispered.

"Look at it. See how big it is?"

"Wow!" Greg said. "That's the biggest lizard I've ever seen!"

"We have to catch it!" Talley said. "I may just keep it!"

"Keep a lizard? Forever?" Greg said loudly.

"Shh," Talley said. "Give me a thread."

Greg looked down. His sock was hanging loose around his ankle.

"I don't have any more threads," he said.

"You have another sock, don't you? Hurry up!" Talley snapped her fingers.

Greg bent over to pull a thread.

"Next you'll want my shirt!" he mumbled.

"Oh, rats!" Talley said. "You were too slow. It got away. I'm going after it. Bring the bag."

"Why don't you carry it?" Greg asked.

Talley was gone.

Greg pulled his socks up and started after her.

Talley climbed over rocks and through bushes. "I've got him!" she whispered. "Hurry up with that thread."

"I dropped it," Greg said.

"Get another one. Hurry!"

Greg put down the bag. He tugged at a thread in his sock.

"Here," he said. "And that's all!"

"If I catch this guy, I won't need any more," Talley said.

"Do you promise? We can go home when you catch this one?"

"I promise," she said.

"Then I'll help," Greg said.

Talley made the loop in the thread.
She reached over the lizard's neck.
It darted off the other way.
"After him!" Talley ran across
the stream.
Greg followed. "Wait for me.
I'm carrying the lizards, you know."
When Greg crossed the stream,
his foot slipped into the water.
His sneaker got wet.
Talley hopped back the other way.
"Will you make up your mind?"
Greg said.
Talley hid behind a bush.
"Over here," she whispered.

Give up!" he said. A squishy noise came from his wet sneaker.

"I've got to have this lizard," Talley said.

Greg said, "I'm all wet."

"Up the cliff, after the blue belly," she said.

"But Talley . . . " Greg said.

Talley was on top, looking down on him.

"I can't climb up," Greg said.

"I've got this bag of lizards."

"Bring it along," she said.

"The climb won't hurt them!"

5. The Chase

Greg climbed to the top. His foot was cold inside his wet sneaker.

"Talley, can we go back now?" he called.

Talley was under a bush. "Not yet. There he goes! After him!"

"You'll never catch it," Greg said. "That lizard is too smart!"

"Quick—give me a thread,"

"Not again!" Greg moaned.

Talley snapped her fingers. Greg sighed. "Why do I listen to you?" He bent over and pulled another thread from his sock. Talley slipped it over the lizard's neck.

"I've got it!" Talley shouted.

"Look!" Greg shouted. "It *is* a blue belly!"

Just then the lizard flipped out of the noose and ran away.

"Look at that—and I had it, too!" Talley moaned.

Greg shook his head. "I thought you were an expert."

"A prize lizard gone! Help me find it," Talley said. She looked around. Greg looked around too. They were above the waterfall. The stream was a long way down.

"How did we get here?" Talley asked. "Where are we?"

"We are in a canyon, lizard hunting," Greg said. "And we're lost. I told you we would be."

Talley said, "Which way do you think the blue belly went?"

"Forget the blue belly." Greg sat down on a rock. "What we need is the Mountain Search and Rescue Team!"

RST
TIONAL
ANK

6.
Lost Forever!

Talley sat down next to Greg. "I'm hungry. Got any food?"

"Just two juicy lizards." Greg handed her the bag.

"They're jumping around in the bag," Talley said.

"Rub their bellies. They'll go to sleep," Greg said.

“I want that blue belly,” Talley said.

“Is that all you can think about?” Greg asked. “How is the Mountain Search and Rescue Team going to find us?”

“Don’t worry,” Talley said, jumping up. “After I catch the blue belly, I’ll get us out.”

“No!” Greg said. “I’m not listening to you again. I’m getting out of here now.” Greg got up and started walking.

"Wait!" Talley said. "What if we get more lost?"

"I'll find a way," he said. "Follow me. And don't forget the bag of lizards!"

7. Where Are We?

Greg found a way off the ledge.
It was a narrow rock bridge
with a long drop on both sides.
"How do we get across?" Greg asked.
"Balance with your arms and run
across," Talley said.
"If I run, I'll trip on my
socks," Greg said.
"Go on," Talley said. "I'm right
behind you."

Greg balanced over the bridge. Talley followed. The bag of lizards hung in her hand.

"We made it!" he said.

They came to a dirt hill.

"We didn't come up this way," Greg said, "but this looks like an easier way down." He slid down the hill.

"Come down, Talley," he called. "And don't squash the lizards!"

At the bottom, Talley was coated with dirt. The bag of lizards was unharmed.

"Well, we got down," she said.

"We aren't out yet," Greg said.

Talley looked around uncertainly.

"Which side was the stream on when we came in? Left or right?"

"Who knows?" Greg said. "We hopped back and forth so many times I lost track."

"Let me think," Talley said.

"The stream was on our left when we got the first lizard."

"Yeah, and my foot got wet when we got the second," Greg said.

"Or was that when we were after the blue belly?" He looked at Talley.

Talley said, "Greg, I think we're lost!"

8.
Help!

"Help!" Greg shouted.

"No one can hear you," Talley said.

"Why not?"

"The trees cut off all noise."

"Talley!" Greg was angry. "If we ever get out of here, I'll never listen to you again!"

Talley wasn't listening.
She licked her finger and
held it up to the wind.
Then she turned around.
"This is the way," she said.
"You're wrong," Greg said.
"We should go downstream."
"Which way is downstream?"
Talley asked.
"We can find out," Greg said.
"I remember something I read in
the paper."
He pulled a leaf off a bush. Then
he dropped it into the water.

It floated with the current
downstream.
"There it goes," Greg said.
"Let's follow it."

9.
No More Socks

Greg ran downhill,
staying next to the stream.
He was stepping on his socks.
He stopped and pulled them up.
They wouldn't stay.
"My socks are ruined!" he yelled.
Talley was behind him, carrying
the bag of lizards.

When she caught up, Greg pointed to the clearing ahead. They could see their bikes.

"Hey, you did get us back!" Talley said. "And we still have the lizards."

"I wish I still had my socks,"

Greg said. They walked to the clearing.

"We have time to stop at the pet store," Talley said. "Tomorrow we can come back for the blue belly."

"Not me," he said. "Why should I ?"

"I need you," Talley said.

"The only thing you need is my socks!"

"Well, they do have good strong threads in them."

"Not any more," he said.

"I'll buy you another pair with my lizard money," she said.

"Say you'll come."

Greg held his ears. "I'm not listening."

"You saved us today," Talley said. "That was really smart, dropping that leaf in the water. You should be on the Mountain Search and Rescue Team!"

"Yeah!" Greg said. "I'd like that."

"You could practice, while I search for lizards," Talley said.

"Okay, I'll come," Greg said. "You search, and I'll rescue."

"It's a deal." Talley got on her bike and rode off. "And don't forget to wear a new pair of socks!"

FIR
NAT
BA

About the Author

NANCY ROBISON is the author of two other Fun-To-Read books, *UFO Kidnap!* and *Space Hijack!* She lives with her husband and four boys in San Marino, California, near where *The Lizard Hunt* takes place. She says, "When one of our boys caught a blue belly lizard, I inadvertently let it go. That was many years ago but he's still looking for it!"

About the Artist

LYNN MUNSINGER illustrated her first children's book in 1978, and since then has illustrated four more. She earned her B.A. from Tufts University and her B.F.A. from the Rhode Island School of Design. Born in Greenfield, Massachusetts, she now lives in South Londonderry, Vermont.